FATHER

TERRY

MOTHER

BROTHER

GARDENER

GRANDMA

LE CHEF

MAID

Then the Troll Heard the Squeak

BY KEVIN HAWKES

LOTHROP, LEE & SHEPARD BOOKS   NEW YORK

to Karen

Library of Congress Cataloging in Publication Data. Hawkes, Kevin. Then the troll heard the squeak / by Kevin Hawkes.   p.   cm. Summary: Little Miss Terry wreaks havoc by jumping on the bedsprings at night, until a troll appears to set things aright. ISBN 0-688-09757-X. —ISBN 0-688-09758-8 (lib. bdg.) [1. Trolls—Fiction. 2. Behavior—Fiction. 3. Stories in rhyme.] I. Title. PZ8.3.H288Wh 1991 [E]—dc20   90-6520 CIP AC

Little Miss Terry
thought it quite merry
to jump on the bedsprings at night.

"Gadzooks!" cried her mother.

"All gone," sighed her brother.

Grandma's new dentures took flight!

The maid took a slip...

...the gardener a clip.

"Oh la la!" cried the cook. "Where's the light?"

Then the troll heard the squeak

and came up for a peek

to set little Miss Terry aright.